SWEET ANNIE

by kaylin rasmussen booker

illustrated by
shiela alejandro

Annie Elizabeth
Calloway Kate
was a sweet little girl
with an unusual fate.
Every morning she awoke in her bed,
with dreams still dancing around in her head.

She'd rub her eyes
and turn to her sister,
then give her a squeeze
before she kissed her.
After a minute she'd quietly say,
"Go ahead, tell me,
what color today?"

See, Annie was born
with a small little tuft
of strawberry hair,
just barely a fluff.
But then one day,
a perplexing thing,

Each morning that followed was a bigger surprise.
Her parents were baffled, but soon realized,
Annie was blessed or enchanted or cursed
with hair that could change for better or worse.

Some days it was straight and black as ink.
Others it curled in tight little kinks.
Purple and green, rainbow and blue,
by 5-years-old she'd worn every hue.

Her hair was discussed
at the breakfast table.
She tried to avoid it
but never was able.

At church
all the ladies
would stop and
fuss about just
how lucky
she really was!

Annie didn't mind
the changing of color,
even when it morphed
from shiny to duller.

She knew it
was something
that set her apart.
She just wished
she was known
more for her heart.

Annie loved dreaming, drawing, and dance.
She loved helping friends when she had the chance.
If someone was sad she'd give them a hug,
make them a card or read them a book.

Her smile was contagious, at least it would be,
if people could look past her hair to see
how joyful she was in every way
no matter the color of her hair that day.

One afternoon
Annie went with her mom,
to visit Miss Peggy
at the nursing home.
They found her sitting
in the main living room,
humming a tune
while working a loom.

"Annie!" She sang
like her name was a song.
"I was hoping your mom
would bring you along!"
"Here, come sit with me,
and I'll teach you to weave."
"I've been learning how
from a show on TV."

Annie sat with Miss Peggy
while they worked on their mastery
of weaving a sweet little
homemade tapestry.

Before she knew it an hour was gone.
Her mom decided it was time to go home.

Her mom brushed her locks over her shoulder, forgetting for a moment that they looked golder. She wrapped Annie up in a great big hug, thinking how precious her little girl was.

"Annie, your heart for others is sweet, but most families must work during the week."

"Well, I don't have to work," Annie declared.
"I've got tons of time that I can share!
Do you suppose that Miss Peggy's friends,
would like for me to visit them?"

"I can't do much,
but I can play rummy,
and my chocolate chip cookies
are pretty yummy.
I could draw pictures, and put on a show!"
Her list of ideas continued to grow.

That night Annie's mom
called the nursing home staff
to ask for permission,
and they simply laughed.

"Of course!
We'd love that sweet little girl
to spend time with us
and brighten our world."

Now every weekday
she goes for a visit
to see all her friends,
no she wouldn't miss it.

They play lots of cards.
She brings snacks to share.
They tell her their stories
and she treats them with care.

And no one ever ever
mentions her hair.

Sweet Annie is based on the true story of a little girl
named Annie with beautiful red hair
and an even more beautiful heart.